MW00931530

# Clarissa's
# Heart

## LATTER-DAY DAUGHTERS

BOOKS IN THE LATTER-DAY DAUGHTERS SERIES

# Clarissa's
# Heart

LATTER-DAY DAUGHTERS

## Launi K. Anderson

Published by
Deseret Book Company
Salt Lake City, Utah

*To Scott, Steve, and Ray,*
*for the tender, loving, and kindly spirit*
*it takes to lead us all forward*

© 1998 Launi K. Anderson

All rights reserved. No part of this book may be reproduced in any form or by any means without permission in writing from the publisher, Deseret Book Company, P. O. Box 30178, Salt Lake City, Utah 84130. This work is not an official publication of The Church of Jesus Christ of Latter-day Saints. The views expressed herein are the responsibility of the author and do not necessarily represent the position of the Church or of Deseret Book Company.

Deseret Book and Cinnamon Tree are registered trademarks of Deseret Book Company.

This book is a work of fiction. The characters, places, and incidents in it are the product of the author's imagination or are represented fictitiously.

**Library of Congress Cataloging-in-Publication Data**

Anderson, Launi K., 1958–
    Clarissa's heart / by Launi K. Anderson.
        p.    cm. — (The Latter-day daughters series)
    "Cinnamon Tree."
    Summary: While traveling from Iowa to Utah with her family and a company of Mormon pioneers in 1856, Clarissa trades a prized treasure for food to nourish her sick little brother.
    ISBN 1-57345-416-8
    [1. Mormons—Fiction. 2. Frontier and pioneer life—Fiction.]
    I. Title. II. Series.
PZ7.A54375Cn    1998
[Fic]—dc21                                    98-33731
                                                    CIP
                                                    AC

Printed in the United States of America          21239-6416

10  9  8  7  6  5  4  3  2  1

"In this life we each have our individual handcarts to push and pull. Yours may be loaded differently than mine and the distance we travel may vary. But we all do have them. During those difficult times, it is good to know we can rely on each other. Most importantly we have the Lord, and we must trust in him to see us through."

PRESIDENT MARK P. ALLRED
*Orem Utah Timpview Stake*

# CONTENTS

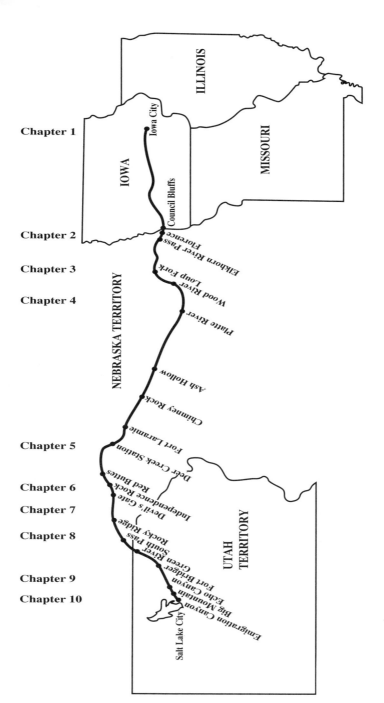

# PROLOGUE

The young man let the other elders pass as he waited by the side of the trail. Pulling at the reins, he nudged his horse around to face the sleeping town below. The sun had not yet edged its way over the mountain crest behind him. Still, it was a warm morning.

Nearly a year had passed since nineteen-year-old Eli Larsen had taken his first look at the Great Salt Lake Valley. He'd shared his westward journey with a wagon train full of converts much like himself. Though he felt a bit anxious, his heart was full of hope for the new life ahead.

See the glossary at the end of this book for an explanation of unusual words and expressions marked with an asterisk (*).

Being young and strong, he and several others had been allotted a large parcel of land in Bountiful, where Brigham Young himself had set them apart as sheep ranchers. The wool crop looked promising when the mission call came. Although it would be three years before he returned to this valley, he knew life would be good here. Still, something was missing.

Holding the linen handkerchief to his lips, he closed his eyes and breathed in. Perhaps it was only his imagination, but for a moment, he was certain the dainty, white cloth held a faint scent of lavender. A smile passed over his face.

Clicking to his horse, he galloped back to join his company. This time he was heading *east*.

## CHAPTER ONE

# Iowa City, Iowa

## 1,306 MILES TO SALT LAKE CITY

My mother loved rain. She would stand there in the tall grass beside the back stoop, with her eyes closed and her face tipped to heaven. She would just let it fall down on her until Father would call, "Emily, come in. You'll be taken ill." She loved not just the sound of it splashing and soaking into the roof but the tired, musty scent that fell with it. "Like the angels are dusting the whole world at once," she'd say.

And Father's voice. She loved that too. Sometimes at night, long after I should have been asleep, I'd hear him singing soft and low, just for her. And I knew how she'd be smiling, as if I were standing right there watching them.

I remember her long, dark curls brushing against my cheek as she wove sprigs of lavender into my hair. I remember her smooth, slim fingers holding onto my hand and her cool lips kissing my forehead. And me. I remember my mother loved *me*.

I awoke with the same start that I had felt each morning for the past three days, feeling the train jolt and rumble beneath me. My whole body ached. It seemed that before we reached Iowa City, I'd be rattled to pieces. Smiling, I thought that sounded like something my brother would say.

Andrew's head slid off my shoulder, making him nod and jerk back, then rest it once again where it had been before. Outside the window the last few stars still shone through the dark sky. I knew that behind us, the sun was on its way up.

Father stirred. "I'd give half a crown* for one night's sleep on a feather bed," he said, stretching.

I rubbed at my neck. "This will be the softest place we sleep for some time. You're not having second thoughts about all this now, are you?"

"No, just a sore back. Look, we came through

4

the sea voyage from England nicely, didn't we?
Even made a few friends." He nodded
at the tiny shell bird that was dangling
around my neck.

Out of habit I reached up and
touched the chain, then looked at the
floor, surprised that after fourteen years he could
still embarrass me so easily.

As though not noticing, he went on. "Then
we survived a year in dirty old Boston. I figure if
we've made it this far, we can't turn back now. At
least not until the boy has seen his buffalo."

"It *is* on his list, after all," I said.

"For Andrew's sake, then."

With my most serious look I said, "Of
course."

I stared out the window at the gray-green
prairie. If not for the occasional clump of sage-
brush whipping past, we would appear to be
hardly moving at all.

"Father," I said, "do you think Aunt Polly has
already gone ahead to the Valley?"

"She may have done. Look how anxious *we've*
been to gather there. She joined the Church a

year before we did. I'm surprised she didn't go long before now."

"Her last letter says if all goes well, she can expect to leave with the rest of the Saints sometime in June."

"Yes," Father said, "but we've no way of knowing which company she's in."

I sighed. "I just hoped that maybe she'd . . ."

Rethinking my words, I suddenly stopped in mid-sentence.

Father knew. "What, wait for us?"

Without looking up, I nodded.

"It's all right, love. You've needed some female company for a long time, haven't you? All we can do is wait and see."

Now it was his turn to stare out the window. I wondered if he was as anxious as I was to see my mother's little sister. It was hard to tell.

The train pulled into Iowa City just after dinnertime. Andrew hopped about on the platform, disappointed already. "So," he said, "where are the Indians? I don't see any Indians."

He was hard to ignore, but we did try.

We reclaimed our luggage and found the

black case where Lillibeth sat inside, waiting. As I lifted the box down, she slipped her paw through the bars and pulled at my dress.

Captain Bennett and his counselors met us at the station. He was a nice-looking man with the same light brown hair as Father, only without the gray edges.

"Dr. Galloway," he said, shaking Father's hand. "How good to meet you. We are so pleased to have your family join our company. Not many have the privilege of traveling with their own doctor."

The other men nodded, taking Father's hand in turn. They introduced themselves to Andrew and me as Brother Perkins and Brother Huffman.

Captain Bennett seemed very young to be the leader of the whole company, but I saw wisdom in his eyes that was older than all of us. He reminded me of the Prophet Joseph, though I'd never seen him. So it was little surprise to learn that the captain had been a devoted friend to the Prophet while in Nauvoo. He spoke of him with tenderness, saying, "I wait for the day when I can embrace that great man again." I found it easy to trust him from the beginning.

We rode the three miles to Handcart City* in a wagon loaded with not only our belongings but with the supplies that the captain and his men had purchased in town. I kept Lillibeth in her box, though every few minutes she meowed at me to let her out.

Andrew chattered to the leaders, giving them little chance to say anything at all. He read them his list—the one he'd been keeping since we stepped foot in America—of all the sights he expected to see before we reached the Great Salt Lake Valley.

"Indians, snakes, buffalo, scorpions, coyotes, bears, wolves, porcupines, skunks . . ." he read, looking around every few words, in case he might be missing something already.

In truth, everything on Andrew's list made me nervous.

Brother Perkins said, "Your sister doesn't look as anxious to see all these sights, ay?"

I gave him a half-hearted smile and said, "I hope to miss it all, sir."

Brother Huffman took great interest in my brother and helped him think up a few more not-so-frightening things for his list. I was tempted to warn the man that he might get more than he bargained for in befriending Andrew.

The camp was different than I imagined it would be. In my worry, I expected more noise and confusion. I was pleased to find that, from what I could see, the camp was a picture of order and calmness, with each family working their own fires and tending to the business of camp life.

Large, round group tents were set up in a great circle, which enclosed the few mules, cattle, and oxen our company had. The men worked at building handcarts,* while the women and children gathered fuel, tended babies, and cooked the food.

Brother Perkins, though obviously a tall, sturdy man, seemed to have more kind and gentle ways than most Americans I'd seen so far. He took us to company tent number two, saying that this was to be our new home while we journeyed, along with four other families. After leaving our belongings stacked in one corner, we went back outside.

Father, Andrew, and I stood together, silent and unsure of what our next move should be. From out near one of the fires, a woman with hair as red as mine arose and came toward us. I paid her little mind until I saw my father's look of surprise.

He whispered my mother's name: "Emily."

All at once the woman smiled. It took my breath away. She looked just like my mother.

"John," she called, making her way to us.

Father shook his head, holding out his arms to her. "Polly, is it really you? Why, Clarissa and I were just saying . . ." He laughed.

She stepped into his embrace and kissed his cheek. "John, how wonderful to see you at last." Leaning back, she looked into his eyes and hugged him again.

Andrew nudged my side. "Who's that?" he asked.

Without taking my eyes off of them, I said, "Andrew, this is our Aunt Polly."

## CHAPTER TWO

# Crossing Iowa

We didn't stay in the camp for long. Once the carts were built, it was time to weigh our things and pack them into the carts.

"Seventeen pounds of baggage each?" I asked.

"It sounds like plenty," Father said, setting Aunt Polly's diamond quilt with the rest of our belongings, "until you remember that dishes, pots, and whatever else you have is also counted as baggage. Not just clothing."

"I'm suddenly glad we left so much in England," I said. "Aunt Polly told me of a family a few weeks back that couldn't take their violins because they were over the weight limit. I can't imagine just leaving something like that by the side of the road."

Lillibeth curled herself around Father's leg.

"You're just lucky that we don't have to weigh your cat," he said.

I picked her up as if to protect her from being left behind. "Oh, she'll follow us. Don't you worry."

Aunt Polly stood just beyond the fires, wrapping the cooking kettle in her spare work dress. She set the bundle down and combed her fingers through her hair. Bending forward, she gathered the tresses* and twisted them into a tight rope. Then, tugging one end piece through the coil, she made a knot that stayed in place even when she took her hand away. *How did she do that?* I wondered.

From somewhere in my memory, I knew this very scene by heart; only it was my mother that I'd seen do her hair up this same way. It felt like she was right there, warming me from the inside out.

Father tried to act as though he had only a mind for his work, but I noticed him watching her as well.

"Don't you think she's beautiful, Father?"

Without looking up, he said, "Yes. Of course I do, love. Though she *is* considered excess baggage."

For just a moment my mouth hung open in disbelief, "Father, why would you ever . . ." Then I realized we were not speaking of the same subject.

I set Lillibeth on top of the clothing pile.

"I don't mean the cat," I said, coming around to his side of the cart. "Perhaps I should be more precise. Don't you think Aunt Polly's beautiful?"

Curiously enough, he said nothing. Even with the June heat upon us, I could see color quickly rising in his face—color that didn't come from the sun.

"What's this?" I teased. "Have I made *you* blush finally?"

Wagging a finger at me, he said, "No more of that. I'll not have you playing old gooseberry* with my life, young lady."

I could see it was best to leave him be. So, changing the subject, I said, "The handcarts are smaller than I expected."

13

He stood up straight. "Suppose that means less to pull, hmmm? I'm sure we'll be grateful by this time next week."

The carts looked like the peddler wagons* back home in England, with a box on two wheels and a pull bar in front. I wondered if Father would be tempted to call, "Fresh fish—cod and herring!" as we paraded through town.

Later, Andrew read his list to Aunt Polly—and to my dismay, she told him that she'd love to see all these awful things as well.

Staring into her face, he said, "You are the bravest lady in the *whole* world."

She just laughed and ruffled his hair.

The next day, Sunday, we attended meetings from morning until late afternoon. We had our hands full just trying to keep Andrew quiet.

Brother Perkins spoke first, giving a lovely speech on working together and helping each other. When he spoke, his lips did their best to hold a calm, serious pose, while his eyes smiled merrily on, as if they couldn't help themselves.

The second counselor, Brother Huffman, spoke next, saying that we must have order and discipline if we are to succeed. At first he acted like a stern, hardened man of rules, but as he bore his testimony to us, his face softened and great tears rolled down his cheeks.

Of course the captain gave the closing remarks. His words touched the hearts of old and young alike, and even Andrew sat motionless. When he spoke of his love for the Savior, I had the feeling that he truly knew him. It gave me a feeling of great peace.

After the meeting, Father and Andrew walked around talking to the other members, while Aunt Polly and I sat together. She turned to me and lifted the gold chain and held up the tiny bird.

"This is such a lovely necklace, Clarissa. Did you bring it from home?"

"No," I said, smiling. "A young man made it for me on our voyage to America."

"Was he part of your group?" she asked.

"He was the captain's son. We became good friends."

"Oh, I see."

"We received a letter from him right after we

got to Boston saying he had joined the Church. We've heard nothing since."

Eli's face drifted through my mind. Beneath a dark seaman's cap, his eyes glittered blue—just like the ocean he seemed tied to. My heart jumped as his smile appeared clearly in my mind. Such a nice smile. It was not easy to forget.

It was Brother Huffman's job to wake us each morning at 5:00 with a shrill blast from his bugle. He took such joy in this task I got the feeling he'd have been happier only if he could fire off a cannon instead.

At any rate, this first morning Andrew, who usually slept like a winter bear, sat straight up, shouting, "Man overboard!"

Father, still buried in his bedroll, could be heard chuckling beneath the blanket. Tossing the covers away, he lit the lamp, took Andrew by the shoulders, and tried to lay him back down.

"Take it easy, Son. We've got them all back in the boat." He winked over at me. "Never fear."

One by one we ventured out into the dark morning. After a hasty breakfast of toasted bread and bacon, we found our place in the line of carts. Aunt Polly stood beside Father at the front while Andrew and I took to the back.

Captain Bennett stood on the tongue* of the supply wagon and gave us last-minute instructions and a prayer. Then, waving his hat, he shouted, "Brothers and sisters, Zion awaits!"

And with that, we were off.

From the start, we'd been told that crossing the mild grasslands of Iowa would prepare us for the rest of the trek. Much of the land was flat, and what hills we found were small. Our muscles would become strong before we reached the fearful mountains farther west.

The people of Iowa seemed to find us an odd-looking lot. Some waved and cheered, while others stood silent, glaring as if we were a band of horse thieves. Still others refused to have any dealings with our group at all. They took every chance to humiliate and scorn us as we passed by.

"Go on," they'd shout. "The Mormons can sure use your help with their grasshopper war!"*

A few were even bold enough to throw old fruit and vegetables at us.

"Father, why must they torment us so?" I asked. "Surely they can see we mean them no harm."

"Pay no mind, family," Father said. "This taunting isn't so different from what we had back home, is it?"

Andrew piped up, "It is, to be sure. They're pitching food at us! See here, I have green mash all over my shirt!"

His eyes glared back at the young rascals who stood shouting all manner of vile things, even as their parents stood by.

Just outside one small town, we came to a dark forested area and stopped at the banks of a shallow stream. It was only about a foot deep, so we thought little of it. Father and the other men continued to pull the carts through the water while the ladies helped children remove their shoes.

A Welsh family's little boy saw something moving in one of the big trees. Before anyone could stop him, he grabbed up a river rock and flung it into the branches of the tallest one.

A terrific howl rang out as if the child had struck a coyote. Within seconds, a dozen boys came raining out of the trees and dashed off toward town. One of them stopped only to rub a red mark on his knee.

Many of the people started to clap.

Aunt Polly stood with her hands on her hips, watching with a satisfied look on her face. Seeing that I was confused, she said, "This happens often. The boys like to hide in the trees waiting for the ladies to cross the river. If we lift our skirts in order to stay dry, the silly rascals think they've had a real show."

Appalled, I watched the boys in the distance, wishing I'd been quick enough to throw a rock myself and pleased that someone else already had.

Andrew took to the Welsh boy, Chris, from the moment the stone left his hand. Though neither knew the language of the other, they became fast friends.

After only a few days, Andrew chattered, "Chris found a dead rattlesnake. I crossed it off my list, but we still want to find a live one. Chris hopes we get attacked by Indians too." And on and on.

One night at supper, after Andrew was asleep, I asked, "How is it that those two spend hours on end together, when neither can understand the other?"

Father poked at the coals and said, "They may not speak the same language, but I assure you they understand each other."

Aunt Polly spooned gravy over a piece of fry cake* and passed a plate to me saying, "When two people have one heart, sometimes no words are needed."

Father's eyes drifted over to Aunt Polly and lingered there until he realized that I was watching him. Then, acting as though he needed water, he coughed and walked into the darkness.

The sparks from the fire floated above us while the smoke swirled into my face. I'd grown used to sore, watering eyes, sooty clothes, and ashes in my food, but it took longer to adjust to the dirt. At least the smoke filled some purpose in that it kept the hungry mosquitoes away. But I could find no useful quality whatsoever in all the dust and dirt we encountered daily.

Brother Huffman said, "Each of us will eat five pounds of dirt before we die, so we'd best get to it," but I found little comfort in that.

## CHAPTER THREE

# Florence, Nebraska

1,031 MILES TO SALT LAKE CITY

It took our company a full three weeks to cross the state of Iowa. My arms had grown more muscular with each day's effort, but they ached so badly at night that I found it hard to sleep.

The blisters on my hands soon became thick, brown calluses—which at any other time of my life would have horrified me. But I soon found that they greatly helped guard against splinters, which could make pushing or pulling that much more difficult.

Since it was the hot season of the year, everyone wore hats and bonnets. They covered our heads well enough but did little to shield our faces from the afternoon sun. Within just a few days, poor Andrew's mouth became so chapped and raw that Aunt Polly put a tallowed cloth* over his bottom lip to keep it from burning further. He was a sight.

We approached Council Bluffs with joy, knowing that fresh water and supplies would be there and that rest was at last just ahead. While still a mile or so out, a rider on horseback approached us, spoke with Captain Bennett, then rode back to the fort.

The captain announced that we would not be allowed to enter the town. Council Bluffs had somehow gotten information that our company was infected with smallpox, which was, of course, not true.

Father said, "Let me go give them my word as a doctor that we are healthy."

It was no use. They would not let us near the place. Instead, we were made to camp on the banks of the Missouri River.

That evening, Aunt Polly asked, "Where's Lillibeth tonight?" I stood and glanced over the camp. "She was napping on the wash pile. I don't see her now."

"Maybe she fell in the river," said Andrew.

"She'll turn up," I said, squinting my eyes at him.

Just after breakfast the next morning, she pranced in.

"Well," I said, scolding, "you had me a bit worried."

"You'd best put her in the case for now," Father said. "She isn't likely to enjoy the water ride."

He was right. We brought our carts and wagons aboard a large ferry* and crossed the

Missouri River in style. Lillibeth cried so loud from her box that I was afraid she would hurt herself.

Florence, Nebraska, was not the great city I had imagined. In fact, the only real things to see were a mill and a large storehouse. We camped on the outskirts for three days, giving everyone a chance to catch up on the washing, mending, and such. Most of the men repaired cart wheels and broken boxes, but Father spent the better part of one day back in the town itself.

Aunt Polly, scrubbing Andrew's shirt, stood up

straight, letting the soapy wash water drip back into the tub. "Aside from the blisters and back-aches," she said to me, "your father hasn't had too much doctoring to do."

"We're lucky," I said. "Sometimes he can be away for days. There was a bit more sickness on the voyage over. We had a bout of typhoid.* My friend Eli almost died."

I poured another kettle full of steaming water into the washtub. Aunt Polly pushed the clothes down with a wooden paddle. With just a hint of a smile on her lips, she said, "And your father's doctoring saved him?"

I tried to make her look at me, but she wouldn't. "Well, yes. Not so much with medicine, but they gave him a blessing. I'm sure that's what did it."

"What a clever fellow," she said. "To save your Eli, I mean."

I reached over and flicked a small bit of water on her arm. Finally, she met my gaze, and we laughed.

Father proved himself to be a clever fellow indeed. He returned to camp carrying a good-sized parcel, looking very pleased with himself. He handed it to Aunt Polly.

She unwrapped it carefully and looked inside. "Cheese, apples, butter, and eggs. John, however did you manage it?"

"It seems they haven't had a doctor near here for months," Father said. "I simply spent the day treating bunions,* cankers, croup,* what have you. They knew that cash money would do me little good, so I ended up with whatever they had too much of."

Our cart was packed much heavier now, being loaded with flour, bacon, sugar, and rice. From here on out, there would be no villages or towns to find supplies in. Only the wilderness lay ahead of us. Before starting out, Captain Bennett sent men to check on the health of the company. The leaders decided that if anyone was too weak to go on, they must stay behind and wait out the season in Council Bluffs.

Sister Hulberg was found unable to push or pull the cart with her husband. She was weak from exhaustion and had fainted three times along the trail. Brother Hulberg was advised to turn back with his wife, his son, Cal, and his baby daughter, Isabelle.

Brother Hulberg was so brokenhearted that he cried, begging the captain to let him stay with the company. Father tried to help as best he could, but Sister Hulberg was so ill there wasn't much he could do for her except agree with the captain. The family left us that afternoon.

That evening, Andrew came walking into camp backwards, dropping small crumbs of Yorkshire biscuits* behind him.

"Andrew," I said, "what on earth are you doing?"

He waved me back with one hand but didn't look up. "Shhhh," he said. "I've almost got him."

Aunt Polly and I exchanged wary glances and said together, "Got who?"

Bumping right into me, he said, "It's for my list."

There, waddling out from a small clump of trees, was a plump ball of prickles heading right for us.

Andrew took his list from his shirt pocket, grinned, and pointed, saying, "Porcupine!"

## CHAPTER FOUR

# Loup Fork

## 917 MILES TO SALT LAKE CITY

Several nights later, we came to the banks of the Loup Fork River. It was the largest and deepest river that we had to cross so far. We camped on the site of an old Pawnee* Indian village.

Brother Huffman took the boys off to a rocky bank and showed them a wonder he'd found completely by accident. Andrew and Chris came back so delighted they were beside themselves.

I half expected them to drop some dead creature's bones beside me or force me to endure another wiggling insect or lizard. But when they each held out a handful of colored beads, I was fascinated right along with them.

Brother Huffman told us that ants often

gather the beads and bury them in their hills. A lucky child digging open the ant hills could sometimes find as much as a cupful of the tiny glass treasures. Aunt Polly spent an evening sewing them onto the boys' shirts so they wouldn't be lost.

Just before dinner one evening, Andrew stood up and pointed to a tiny speck on the road behind us.

"Father, what's that following us?" he asked. "I hope it's a buffalo."

We all stood and looked to where he pointed, but I, for one, couldn't see anything.

A few men were sent back to discover what was actually on the road behind us. When they returned with their report, Captain Bennett took off his hat and scratched through his hair.

At last he said, "We've certainly come too far to have anyone start back now. Go, men, and bring the poor fellow in."

When the men returned a second time, Brother Perkins carried a sleeping baby on his shoulder. Upon closer inspection, I realized that it was little Isabelle Hulberg.

Brother Perkins told us that the family had been following us for the last 50 miles.

"That Brother Hulberg sure is a strong old bear," he said. "Pulled his whole family in the cart all this way. That's grit."*

"Here," I said, reaching up, "let me take the baby."

"Mind, now, she's not too heavy," he said, "but if her ma don't get to feeling better, you may be luggin' this parcel a mighty long way."

Smiling down at the tired little face, tinted pink with sun, I said, "I think we'll manage beautifully."

By ten o'clock the next morning, the leaders were still hard at work trying to figure a way across the river. At the lowest spot, it would be well over Andrew's head.

A few men waded out, but the current was so swift and the bottom so sandy that they lost their footing. Aunt Polly and five other women linked arms and started out, but as the water rose, they began slipping and turned back. Brother Hulberg suggested emptying the carts and pulling them through one at a time. The wagons were then loaded with the supplies from each handcart and hauled back and forth by our sturdy mules. This worked well enough, but it took a long time. Still, we hadn't figured out a way to get all the people across.

Just as the last wagon load of provisions was nearing the far bank, there appeared thirty or more Indian braves, poised on spotted horses as if waiting to have their likenesses* sketched.

"Indians!" yelled Andrew. "I knew we'd find them."

Father took hold of Andrew and pulled him back to his side, saying, "Quiet, Son."

I grabbed the baby and ran behind Father. Aunt Polly stood tall by the riverbank while many of the women hid behind their husbands.

Captain Bennett and his men walked up the hill and spoke to them for what seemed like an hour. When at last they came back, they told us that the braves had agreed to help us across the river on their horses.

I stood clutching Isabelle, looking first at the water and then at the Indians. Part of me wanted to plunge into the river and take my chances at getting across on my own. Though I knew we'd never make it, the idea was far less frightening to me than riding bareback with a native.

The braves rode forward and began pulling willing travelers onto their horses. One of the women was so scared that halfway through the water, she burst into tears.

The Indians were delighted with the women's terror, and some of them whooped and reared their horses back in order to make the women scream all the more.

When Aunt Polly's time arrived, two of the warriors began fighting over her. Just before it came to blows, the shorter of the two turned and stalked off.

The winner tried to help her onto his horse, but she pushed his hand away and pulled herself up in one swift motion. Her daring move just amused him. He reached up and touched her hair, saying a string of words in his own language.

Aunt Polly jerked her red hair from his fingers and gave him a fierce look, saying, "You won't have this scalp."

The brave threw back his head and laughed as if he understood every word she'd said.

It made my skin shiver to stand so near to these frightening men. Aunt Polly acted so brave.

Grabbing a piece of his horse's mane, the Indian mounted and galloped into the water, with Aunt Polly holding on for dear life.

"Father," I whispered.

"It'll be all right, Clarissa," he said. "Give Isabelle to me, and you take Andrew."

My brother, having no idea how terrifying this was for the rest of us, could hardly hold in his excitement. He jumped around as if he could barely wait for his turn.

"Father," I said, "how will you cross with the baby?"

"I'll send her in the wagon, then start over with the men."

Isabelle wailed as he took her from my arms, but I knew she'd be safer in the wagon.

Andrew pulled my arm and pointed, saying, "We should ride with that warrior. He has more feathers than that other one does. Can we go with him?"

"Andrew, please hush," I said, trying to sound calm.

A younger-looking Indian waited off to the side, watching me. When at last I mustered up enough courage to go across, I had but to hold my chin up and take a deep breath, and he rode forward. Reaching one arm around my waist, he lifted me up, as if it was no effort at all, to sit in front of him. I thought he was going to leave Andrew behind, but then he whirled the horse around and scooped him up and sat the boy in back.

It took all the control I had not to scream out when he ran his horse into the icy water. Closing my eyes, I could feel my heart banging inside my ribs. All the while, Andrew hung on, laughing for all he was worth.

As the pony climbed the opposite bank, we slid back but managed to stay on.

Aunt Polly helped me down and nodded a curt "thank you" to the brave.

He slapped his hand on his bare chest and said, "Kiasak."

I stared at him, still feeling shaky from the ride. To be polite, I said, "My name's Clarissa."

Andrew held up his paper, saying, "Indians. Check."

## CHAPTER FIVE

# Chimney Rock

### 578 MILES TO SALT LAKE CITY

"Where's the smoke?" Andrew said. "I don't see any smoke."

I set my hand on his shoulder and tried not to laugh at him. "It's a rock that *looks* like a chimney. It really isn't one."

Luckily, Andrew was able to put another mark on his list when a family of prairie dogs scampered out of the brush. The day wasn't a total loss.

Isabelle's father, still overburdened with his sick wife and small son, came to see and hold the toddler in the evenings. The leaders gave Sister Hulberg permission to ride in the supply wagon, but the boy still walked or rode with his father as best he could.

Just as we were finishing up our supper meal one night, Andrew and Chris came into our camp, petting and poking the horned toads* they had caught. Though I can't bear reptiles, I did feel sorry for these. This was Andrew's third that he'd tried to keep as a pet. They all died—either from being fed the wrong kind of food, from too much handling, or, I'm sickened to say, Lillibeth ate them. Whichever way, the outlook was bleak.

It was on the trail that runs alongside the North Platte River that our food supply began to dwindle. Though my stomach was never really empty, I grew so tired of the thin, flavorless gruel that I prayed nightly for something—anything else. Over and over, the children cried for a bit of meat to go with the porridge or hard biscuits that we ate for days on end.

Brother Folkman, an elderly man, became so frustrated with the scanty food supply that one afternoon he decided to go out after something else.

"Isn't he a bit old for hunting?" Aunt Polly asked.

"No, no," Father said. "On the contrary. He actually killed a wild beast which he thought would make a terrific stew."

"What kind of wild beast?" she asked.

"First, it needs to be said that Brother Folkman is losing his eyesight."

Aunt Polly looked at me.

I shrugged.

"It seems that his sense of smell is gone as well."

"Oh, no." I covered my mouth. "He didn't . . ."

"Yes, the poor old codger* caught himself a full-grown skunk!" Father took out his handkerchief and wiped his eyes, but he still wasn't finished laughing.

"Is he poisoned?"*

"To say the least. He has cleared every area for twenty rods* around," Father said. "The sad part is, the fellow can't understand why no one will come near him or cook his meat!"

"Perhaps Andrew can check off 'skunk' without actually having to see it," Aunt Polly said. "The smell should be enough."

By the end of the week, Brother Folkman was still walking at the back of our company because of his terrible smell. He was given supplies and left with his grown son at Deer Creek Station. Though the old fellow didn't want to stay, his son assured the captain that he would keep his father there until the spring, when he had completely "aired out."

The captain came to our tent before breakfast one morning to talk to Father. They stood just far enough away that neither Aunt Polly nor I could hear what they were saying. Father came back in the tent, smirking like he had heard a good joke, but just went ahead making up his bedroll.

"John," Aunt Polly said. "What is it?"

His smile grew wider until finally he said, "It seems your friends have returned."

I looked up. "What friends?"

"The Indians who brought you two across the river. Clarissa, you remember Kiasak. And Polly,

39

your fellow's name is Pauchu. It appears they've been asking about you."

"What?" Aunt Polly said.

I stood, making ready to hide. "Where are they?"

Father didn't act a bit concerned. "Oh, they've gone back to their village."

"What do they want?" I said.

Father scratched through his whiskers. "The captain's not sure, but it appears that they are trying to make a bargain."

Together Aunt Polly and I shouted, "For what?!"

At that, Father tried to look serious.

"Understand, ladies, these people have never seen women with hair the color of fire. In truth, they are quite fascinated by the two of you."

I grabbed a handful of hair and tossed it off my shoulder, as if that would protect it somehow. "They want our hair?"

"No, no, dear," he said. "They want *you*."

"John!" Aunt Polly came one step closer to Father, then stopped. There wasn't much that ruffled her, but this plainly did. "You've got to do something. I mean, shouldn't you? What did the captain say?"

"He told them that we don't trade our people like blankets and that under no circumstances would he consider this sort of barter. He felt certain they understood." Then, with a grin, he said, "Of course, his *Pawnee* is a bit rusty."

"Father," I said, keeping my voice as steady as possible, "how can you think this is funny?"

"Well, I must admit," he was grinning outright now, "the idea of the two of you running off to become Indian squaws was not something I'd given much thought to."

"And you shouldn't now, either," Aunt Polly said.

Seeing that she was not smiling and I was close to tears, he stopped his teasing and said, "Come, come now, you two. They've left, and they won't be back. Don't worry."

"Are you certain?" Aunt Polly said.

"Quite."

I went to the doorway of the tent and looked out toward the trail. *How could anyone be certain?* I wondered.

## Chapter Six

# Independence Rock

### 332 Miles to Salt Lake City

Father promised Andrew that he could carve his name in the mountain along with the others once we came to Independence Rock.* The only trouble was that we arrived there late at night, and no one would climb the rock with him in the dark. He was so sure he could hike it himself that we dared not take our eyes off of him until he was asleep, for fear he'd try it.

I was so relieved the next morning to see that he was still asleep under his usual jumble of blankets. Then, for some reason, I reached down and patted the quilt and found that he wasn't there at all.

Shaking Father's arm, I said, "Wake up. Andrew is gone."

Coming from a dead sleep, he rolled over and growled. "What do you mean he's gone?"

I flipped back Andrew's covers and held my hand out toward the empty bed so that he could see for himself.

Aunt Polly sat up. "You don't think he'd really try to climb that rock alone, do you?"

Sleeping in our clothes did have its advantages at times like this. The three of us sprang out the tent door and headed for the hill.

The early morning sun lit the top of Independence Rock like it was on fire. From where we stood at the bottom, it was hard to tell if anyone was above us. Aunt Polly and I called, "Andrew! Where are you?" while Father made his way around to the other side.

At last we heard a faraway voice sing out, "Here I am! Up here!"

We shielded our eyes against the brightness and finally spotted the little speck that was

Andrew. There he sat, as pleasant as you please, at the top of the hill, with both arms waving at us.

"Don't move," Aunt Polly shouted. "Your father is coming."

He looked down the side behind him and said, "I see him." Then, waving that direction, he yelled, "Hello, Father."

Though Father spoke too quiet for us to hear, we saw enough finger-shaking to know that Andrew was given a good thawing out.*

When at last they both came down, we found a smooth spot and carved our names in the sandy rock. Father put his above mine and Andrew's, and Aunt Polly etched hers at the bottom. Father helped her hold the knife steady, because the area she chose had a hard spot.

His large hand covered hers as they worked, guiding the point over and over the rock. Though tiny beads of perspiration ran down Father's face, Aunt Polly just laughed as her name scrawled out, looking more like a child's writing than Andrew's.

I nudged my brother and whispered, "Let's leave them to finish alone."

"But I don't want to . . ." he tried to say before

I covered his mouth and pulled him away with me. I don't think they even noticed that we left.

We awoke the next morning to the thundering of a thousand animals on the move, quite near our camp. At first we feared it to be a stampede of buffalo. But, to Andrew's disappointment, it turned out to be a herd of wild stallions. There must have been well over a hundred of them galloping past the camp as though we were not there. They were so beautiful.

"Horses?" Andrew said. "I can see horses any time. I'm going back to bed."

It rained heavily that night while we slept. I dreamed of my mother holding Father's hand, standing there in the rain, smiling. Then, on the other side of Father, with the very same smile, stood Aunt Polly.

Our tent did a fair job of keeping out the water, but many of the other people looked like they had spent a miserable night, wet and cold. All we had for breakfast was the hard bread left over from dinner, as everything was too wet to start a fire.

Once we got started, the roads proved to be one long span of sticky mud. Here the people without shoes had the advantage, as it was considerably easier to remove your bare foot from a mud hole than a booted one. What little remained of my own shoes I gladly left below the surface. In truth, the cool, wet mud did feel wonderful to my dry, cracked feet.

Aunt Polly vowed never to complain again about the dust blowing in her face, for as uncomfortable as that had been, this mud was a dreadful trial.

No matter how hard Andrew and I pushed or with what determination Aunt Polly and Father pulled, our cart would sink down sometimes to the hub* instead of going forward. It was a struggle just to free it from the ditches, never mind pulling ahead.

The four of us fell time and time again. Just as one of us would rise, another would go down. If we hadn't been so bone tired and sore, it might have been funny.

Andrew took one quick spill and on his way grabbed my neck and brought me down with him. We didn't even try to get up at first. My dress was too wet and heavy, and I had little strength left.

Just then the captain called a rest halt.

Out of habit I reached up to touch the necklace at my throat. After a second or two, my fingers found the chain, but the carved shell—the pelican—was gone! Holding out my skirt, I tried to see if maybe the little bird was stuck in the mud caked on my dress. I ran my hands over the fabric, but it was not there.

If it had come off while we were pushing the cart, it could be buried in the wet ground, maybe a foot deep.

In complete despair, I slid down and sat beside the handcart, trying my best not to cry.

Andrew plopped down next to me and said, "Hope we meet some trappers soon."

Staring straight ahead, I said nothing.

"When we see some, I'm gonna go right up to them and say, 'I'll make you a trade for that rifle.' And they'll say, 'Good deal.'"

"Andrew," I said. "Please stop."

"Then I'll shoot rabbits and bears and buffalo,

and everyone will say, 'Here comes the greatest hunter in all the land,' and I'll—"

I rested my head in my grimy hand, saying, "We will meet no such character on this road. And if we did, we'd have nothing to trade."

He coughed hard for a few seconds, but it didn't stop his prattle.*

"I'm sure *you* don't. But I certainly do. Got it right here in my pocket. Want to see?"

*No,* I thought.

"Do you?" he said again, this time coming right up into my face.

"Of course, of course. By all means, show me."

He held out his dirty little fist, turned it around and opened it slowly. Just as I suspected, there sat a lump of mud wadded into a ball. I batted my eyes at him in disbelief. "Do you know people who trade for mud, Andrew?"

"Maybe," he said, grinning. "If there's a treasure inside." He began flicking the clay apart with his fingers. *Boys,* I thought, turning away. Before I could become any more irritated with his silly game, he dangled a dirty little stone so close to my face that my eyes saw two. Pushing his arm back, I realized that it wasn't a stone at all.

"My pelican!" I shouted. "Andrew! How did you . . . I don't believe . . . where did you ever . . . ?" Finding no words that fit my joy, I threw my arms around his neck and gave his muddy face a kiss.

"Oh, so now I'm a hero?"

"You certainly are."

"Good then, madame," he said, coughing again. "I'll take my reward in gold nuggets, if you please."

## CHAPTER SEVEN

# Devil's Gate

## 327 Miles to Salt Lake City

By the time we reached the Sweetwater River at the foot of Devil's Gate, Andrew was not himself. His cough had become more shrill and he complained of an aching head.

When Father carried him to bed, Andrew asked, "Please, can I have some broth?" We had nothing to make broth from, so I asked at each of the other tents if anyone had some kind of meat. There was none. So our poor Andrew went without.

In the morning, I rose early with Aunt Polly to help her get breakfast, such as it was.

"You miss him, don't you?" she said. "Your Eli."

I stirred the steaming porridge, wanting to finally talk to someone.

"It's all right, Clarissa. I've watched you with the little shell bird. A person would have to be blind not to see how much the giver means to you."

I nodded. "That's just the problem. I can't have him mean so much to me. There is no sense to it. I've tried to forget him, but sometimes . . ."

My aunt wiped her hands on her apron and sat down next to me. "Sometimes, the people who stay in our minds the clearest are those who have taught us something valuable. Maybe it's best not to forget them."

"But it's certain I'll never see him again."

"Ah," she said, "so few things are ever *certain.* But this I do know. If you are prayerful about all this, it will turn out just the way it should."

Sighing, I said, "I hope you're right."

A hoarse cough came from the tent.

"I'll go see if Andrew can take some porridge," I said. On an impulse, I turned to Aunt Polly and kissed her cheek.

We went six miles that day without water.

Brother Perkins rode on ahead to scout out our next stopping place. When he came at last to the first sign of water, it was in the form of a large buffalo wallow.* Many of the children ran to it, scooped up the mud, and strained the water from it with their teeth. It made me sad to watch them, but at least they were satisfied.

Andrew tried his best to put on a brave front. He walked slow and steady, saying little—which, for him, was a dead giveaway that he felt terrible.

Father checked him at midday, and from then on the boy was pulled in the cart. It was very hard to hear him ask for a cupful of soup and have nothing to give him. If only there was a speck of meat to make broth from.

Sister Hulberg came to our tent to thank us for helping her with Isabelle. At last, there was color in her cheeks, and she looked much stronger. Little Isabelle reached both arms up to her mother, which made the poor woman cry with joy. I knew I would miss the baby greatly.

Late one afternoon, as we approached a particularly hilly road, coming from behind us on the trail were the Indians Kiasak and Pauchu.

My father was about thirty groups up the line with the Hanson family. Their father was ill and there was no one but children to pull their cart.

With Aunt Polly at the front and me at the back of our cart, we did indeed look like two lone women, which made us all the more uncomfortable.

Each of the Indians had a pony tied behind his own horse, loaded down with dozens of blankets.

"Aunt Polly," I called. "What should we do?"

"Sometimes it is best to do nothing," she said, glaring at them.

Our group kept going, but the two men rode along beside us for over an hour. They appeared very curious about the handcarts. Pauchu, the older of them, dismounted at one point and motioned for us to let him try pulling it. With everyone else too afraid to speak, we felt there was no choice but to step aside and let him try.

He was a tall fellow, and his arms and shoulders were muscular beyond that of most of the men in our company, with the exception of Brother Hulberg.

Though he kept up with the other carts in line, it was clear from his appearance that this had not been easy to do. His breathing was heavy—as if he was dragging a buffalo—and great drops of sweat fell from his face. He held onto our cart for a quarter of a mile; then at last he stopped, set down the crosspiece,* and walked back to his horse. He and Kiasak rode ahead and left us to wonder what would happen next.

Looking down at my bare, dirty feet, my shredded dress, and chapped, callused hands, I wondered how anyone could find us attractive, red hair or not.

"Hopefully," I said, "the captain will tell them that we're not interested in being their squaws."

Aunt Polly said, "In their culture, it doesn't matter if the woman is interested. As long as she doesn't belong to anyone, they consider her fair game."*

"Well, *you* belong to us."

"I hope that counts," she said.

Suddenly, Andrew, who had been fast asleep

in the cart, began to cry—something he hadn't done in a very long time.

We pulled off to the side and let the others pass us, while Aunt Polly saw to him.

"What is it, dear?" she asked.

"It hurts in here," he said, pointing to his chest. "It's hard to breathe."

Aunt Polly lifted him out, while I spread the quilt down for him to lie on. Andrew was always such a sturdy soul that it frightened me to hear him breathing in short little bursts.

"He is quite weak," she said. "See if he can take a drink."

I poured Andrew a cup of water from the small barrel we kept in one corner of the cart. But as I held it to his dry, chapped lips, he took a tiny sip and cried out again.

"No—it hurts!"

"I've never seen him like this. He usually tries to be so brave. For him to say something hurts, it must be very bad."

Aunt Polly studied him. "If we were at home,

I'd give him a good dose of saffron tea.* My mother swore by it."

"We need help," I said.

"Your father is at least a mile up the road. He won't even know we've pulled off until they make camp."

"Then we'll have to get help some other way," I said. With that, I knelt down on the quilt beside Andrew and waited while Aunt Polly did the same. We quietly prayed that we would know how to help Andrew.

I was inclined to stay where we were and trust whatever help there was to come to us.

Aunt Polly said, "No. We need to get him to your father. He'll know what to do."

"Couldn't we just wait here?" I said, feeling lazy all of a sudden.

Aunt Polly stood up. "We've got to get back with the group. I've heard tell of a woman who kept wandering away from the company. She was told time and time again to stay with the group, work together, and never prowl around alone. Feeling that she knew better than her leaders, she pulled off on her own one day, supposing to catch up later. But for her, later never came.

"When they set out searching for her that evening, all they found was her bonnet and signs of a wolf ruckus."*

"I don't like the thought of that much," I said.

"That's where the saying 'There is strength in numbers' comes from. Her captain knew it. Ours knows it, and believe me, the wolves do too."

I couldn't say for certain, but it seemed that she and I had a surge of strength about then. We pulled faster than ever and made it to the tail end of our group just as the sun was going down.

## CHAPTER EIGHT

# South Pass

## 232 MILES TO SALT LAKE CITY

With one look at Andrew, Father went right to work. First, he gave the boy an emetic* to break up his cough and next a dose of lobelia* to help him rest. Once the medicines had taken their effect, Andrew slept. We took turns seeing to him throughout the night.

He showed little sign of improvement by morning, but we were pleased to see that at least he was no worse.

That afternoon, while coming through a wide open flatland, there was a strange wave of heat that felt like we were entering an oven. As we came nearer to the bluffs,* the company slowed. Without knowing it, we had walked ourselves right into the path of a prairie fire. It blazed in a steady line right beside our handcart train.

"I've heard about these things," Father said. "They can catch the wind and surround you within a matter of minutes."

Aunt Polly squinted at the line of charred grass off in the distance. "Well, I for one don't think the Lord brought us all the way out here to see us scorched. Now then, we must keep moving or we certainly will be surrounded."

With that, we pushed and pulled all the harder and encouraged the others to do the same. The fire, though still burning low, seemed to stay in the same place all the while we were moving. Someone up ahead began singing the "Handcart Song,"* which gave us the courage to move on. We never dared take our eyes off the searing glow ten rods away from us. Finally, we passed the edge of the fire and hurried the last of the carts out of its path as well. That done, we stood back, astonished, as the blaze swept madly on.

The next morning, there were shouts throughout camp that a supply wagon was headed our way. Our first thought was that it was from Salt Lake, but that was not the case.

We learned for ourselves that the wagon was owned and operated by a man named C. J. Feldman from far-off California. His first aim had been to make his fortune mining for gold, but that having failed, he had found a much better way to become rich.

Every summer, this man would buy up provisions from the towns and forts along the westward trail. Then he and his ugly dog and broken-horned cow would head east and make a fine living selling and trading his goods to the starving pioneers. He took from them whatever they could pay in exchange for fresh supplies.

Needless to say, this vile, dark-eyed fellow was not appreciated among us. However, this did not keep everyone from dealing with him. Having survived on nothing but bread and water for the last few weeks, I felt certain that just looking at something as glorious as a slab of bacon or piece of fruit would do my heart good.

I came to the wagon out of sheer curiosity and found myself there with many others. The people of our company were certainly not rich—just hungry.

Having no way to purchase any of the things we needed so badly gave me a feeling inside like a cold stone was wedged in the pit of my stomach.

I watched Brother Brereton trade his gold watch for two pounds of venison—something that should have cost 25 cents. The sad part was that he was happy to pay it, because his family needed the meat. Likewise, Brother Stott gave up a jeweled hair clip for the opportunity to milk Mr. Feldman's milch cow,* all so that his family could have a cup of milk with their biscuits.

"What do ya need, missy?" Mr. Feldman said, startling me.

I looked at him but could find no words. What did we need? What *didn't* we need? What difference did it make? I had nothing to trade. Nothing . . . nothing but . . .

"That's a might purty necklace you got there, gal."

I reached up and covered the tiny bird with my hand. It made me angry to even have this man looking at it, imagining it could be his to sell to someone else.

"You look like you could use a little meat. Maybe a little salt pork? How 'bout beef steak? Wouldn't that taste good now? How long's it been?"

He kept talking, and I tried not to listen, but when I heard the word *chicken,* he had my interest. He held up a scrawny, half-dead rooster by its feet.

"Now then, missy. What d'ya say? What good's a neck bob* when you're needin' soup? Here, I'll even throw in a couple of carrots." He chuckled.

I thought of Andrew calling for broth, and I remembered the other tired, half-sick people in our company. As skinny as the bird was, it would make a fair pot of soup. But how could I . . . ?

The wretched man came close enough for me to smell the tobacco on his breath. Grinning like the creature he was, he said, "What's it gonna be, missy? I got plenty of folks that can make up their minds."

With my hand still protecting the shell from

his gaze, I closed my fingers tightly around it. I felt cold and sick inside, and my eyes began to sting. Shutting them tightly, I held my head up and whispered, "I'm so sorry, Eli." Then, with one anguished motion . . . I pulled. The delicate chain made a quiet snap and fell broken in my hand. Without opening my eyes, I held my precious treasure out to Mr. Feldman.

He snatched it up and thrust the chicken at me. Feeling a tear run down the side of my cheek, I grabbed the bird from him and ran back to camp.

Aunt Polly never asked how the meat had come to us. She just took it from me and handed it to my father. Then, wrapping both arms around my trembling shoulders, she pulled me to her and held tight. I buried my face in my hands, ashamed to cry over something so small.

But it didn't feel small to me.

"It's all right," she whispered, patting my back. "It's all right."

Her words came in soft, gentle tones that felt like raindrops falling on my tired shoulders. She stroked the back of my hair, then took hold of my arms and pulled me away just enough for me to see her face. Her bottom lip quivered as she said, "I know."

She stayed with me for a little while as I slept in the tent. Soon the smell of chicken broth filled the camp. I could rest a little easier knowing Andrew would have his soup at last.

## CHAPTER NINE

# Echo Canyon

## 66 MILES TO SALT LAKE CITY

Somewhere between Green River and Black's Fork, Andrew became his old self again. Not only was it a relief to have his weight *behind* the handcart instead of *in* it, but Chris was beginning to make a pest of himself, hoping to one day find Andrew well enough to play again. It was with gladness that Father finally pronounced him fit as a fiddle and right as rain.

"It feels like feast or famine to me," Aunt Polly said one morning out of the blue.

Father said, "How's that?"

"First, we cross three waist-high rivers before ten o'clock; then we go fifteen miles with no

water at all. Next, we come to a Roman sandpit.*
At least in England, there was consistency."

She was right. Just as we got used to one type
of ground, it would completely change out from
under us. Many roads were a miserable type.
Some were almost pleasant. But in other places
there was no path at all. Rocks and sand were the
worst.

Lillibeth turned out to be the best trooper of
all. She rode in the cart by day and prowled for
her own food at night. She must have had a feast,
for while we grew lean, she was becoming fat.
Many times I worried that she wouldn't come
back before we left. Then, just as the whistle
would sound, up she'd prance.

At least with Brother Folkman gone, I didn't
worry so much about someone mistaking her for
stew meat.

It was hard not to think about my necklace.
Out of habit, I would occasionally reach up to
touch it, only to find it missing. I felt as if Eli—
or the memory of him—was disappearing, and
nothing I could do would bring it back.

The nights grew colder and colder as we came close to the end of our journey.

As we entered the mouth of Echo Canyon, the worst storm of all fell upon us. There was no time to take shelter or set up tents. The wind was so strong that tents would have blown down or been destroyed anyway. The rain and hail poured on us as if from a pitcher. Soaked clear through from  head to toe, we kept marching until lightning struck a tree across the canyon.

Captain Bennett called a halt and yelled for everyone to climb under the carts and "wait this one out." There we sat, cold and drenched, watching the lightning flash and hearing the thunder around us.

The most terrific scene, though frightening, was to see the supply wagon light up like a bonfire. There were no flames, but the sparks from a lightning bolt hissed and crackled around the metal rims of the wagon wheels two or three times, then went out.

When at last the clouds cleared, we trudged ahead half a mile before finding a wooded cove to make our campsite. By this time, I felt an odd heaviness within my chest, and my eyes ached. Hoping that rest would ease my weariness, I went without dinner and straightaway to bed.

I have little memory of the next few days, other than feeling as though I would burn up one moment or freeze to death the next. I awoke several times to find myself drenched in cold sweat. We may have crossed a dozen rivers, for I had a sense of being carried or pulled across in the cart. My clothes were continually damp, having no chance to dry between the streams and rain showers.

Father gave me the same emetic and lobelia with little results except that afterwards I felt sick to my stomach.

At one point, my head seemed full of voices— whether real or imaginary, I cannot say. Some of the sounds were so distant that they were more like dreams, but others came close enough to make me reach out for them.

I heard Father and Aunt Polly speaking, but

when I opened my eyes, they were not there. I imagined Eli standing next to me, holding out my necklace. How I wanted my arms to reach for it, but they would not move. In my fevered mind I'd see his eyes, hear his voice, and then they were gone. I called to him to stay with me, but no words would come. And so I slept again.

I thought I awoke one morning in a big, beautiful building surrounded by sunlight. My pain was gone, and I felt such joy that I ran from room to room looking for Aunt Polly or Father to show them that I was well. At last, at the end of a long corridor, I saw Aunt Polly. As I came closer, it was not her at all, but my mother. She held her arms out to me, and I wanted so badly to go to her. As I took my first steps, there was a strange, pulling feeling drawing me back . . . back.

The pain in my chest was terrible, and it hurt so to breathe that I could draw only short gasps of air. I shivered so within my feverish body that I could not keep myself still.

Opening my eyes, I knew again that it was only a dream. And yet it felt so real. There, standing above me with their hands upon my head, were my father and . . . Eli. I closed my eyes tight, then opened them again. I forced my mind to hear the words being spoken to me. It was not my father's voice, but the other man's. The one I wished so to be my friend Eli.

He seemed to say, "As elders in Israel, and by the power of the Holy Melchizedek Priesthood which we hold, and in the name of Jesus Christ, we lay our hands upon your head and say unto you, Clarissa Galloway, from this moment on, be ye whole."

Perhaps the only person who could truly know how I felt at that moment would be Lazarus. For, much like the manner in which he came forth out of the tomb, so was I called back from the valley of death.

Immediately the pain and heaviness in my chest were gone, and my head no longer ached. I felt strength flow over my body like a warm stream, from the top of my head clear down to my feet. I opened my eyes and, for the first time in days, saw those standing around me: Father, Aunt Polly, little Andrew, and . . . how could it be? . . . Eli!

Looking into his eyes, I knew I'd either died and was now in heaven, or I had truly been healed. Reaching to my throat, my fingers found the carved shell bird that he'd given me once before. Somehow it was mine again. I had so many questions, but right then they didn't seem important. All I could do was smile and drift off to sleep.

## CHAPTER TEN

# Emigration Canyon

## TEN MILES TO SALT LAKE CITY

"It didn't take long to make out what had happened, Sir," Eli said. "The second I saw Clarissa's necklace hanging in that fellow's wagon, I knew your family was near and in some kind of trouble. As angry as I felt, I didn't have much trouble convincing him to give it to me."

He took a stick and poked it into the fire, letting the tip smolder. Staring at the flames, he smiled, then looked up at me. "As for you, young lady. It's one thing to find you saving scraps for the cat, but it's quite another to have you bartering* with riffraff like Mr. Feldman."

"I'm sorry, Eli," I said. "Andrew was sick, and he needed broth. I had nothing else to trade."

He shook his head so slightly that I might have been the only one who saw, saying, "You did what you had to do, and I'm so grateful. Otherwise, I might have ridden right past your company without knowing you were here. I can't tell you how pleased I am that that didn't happen."

My ladylike senses told me to look away, but I couldn't be coy. I was just too happy. So, doing the only logical thing possible, I smiled back.

"And you made it to the Valley before we did," Father said, shaking his head.

"Yes. After finishing the Book of Mormon you gave me, I was too restless to go back to sea with my father. With his blessing, I set off to find out more about your gospel, and, well, here I am."

Aunt Polly said, "And now you're on your way to England. How long is this mission for?"

Lillibeth, looking surprisingly tired and thin, coiled against Eli's leg. He reached down and lifted her to his lap.

"We've been called for three years, ma'am."

"That's a long time," Father said.

Aunt Polly nodded to me. "Sounds just about right."

"You may just like it in England," Father said.

"Oh, don't you worry," Eli said, his eyes glimmering. "I'll be back. In fact, there is a great deal of cleared land in Bountiful already. You might want to homestead that area. I know the neighbors."

It felt so wonderful to laugh.

Lillibeth jumped down and leaped onto the handcart and disappeared into her box.

"That's the first time she's gone in there without a fuss," Father said.

Aunt Polly went over and peered into the case. She caught her breath. "Well, she has a few very good reasons to go in now." Motioning to me, she said, "Three very good ones."

Andrew and I peered into the case to see the tiny kittens Lillibeth tried to hide from us. She batted her eyes as if not interested but kept one protective paw over her babies. Father said, "Motherhood must suit her. I can hear the purring from here."

Just then, Captain Bennett and his men came into our camp and sat with Father.

"John, you're going to have to think of something. These two just won't stop," he said.

"Who?" Father said.

"The Indians," he said.

Eli leaned toward Andrew and said low, "What's the story here, my friend?"

Andrew, not a bit alarmed, said, "Oh, those Indians are trying to make squaws out of Aunt Polly and Clarissa. All because of their 'fire hair.' But I say hold out till they bring a buffalo to trade. I haven't seen one of them yet."

Eli reached into his shirt pocket. "Will *dried* buffalo count?"

Andrew took the jerky and held it up for a moment, studying it.

"Umm . . . I guess it'll have to do." He then pulled the crumpled list out of his pocket and checked off "buffalo."

Captain Bennett stood.

From around the supply wagon rode the warriors Kiasak and Pauchu. Behind them in the meadow, we saw over a dozen beautiful ponies.

"They think we're just driving a hard bargain," said the captain. "Perhaps if *you* were to tell them."

Father took a deep breath and rose to his feet. "I'll put a stop to this once and for all."

Aunt Polly said, "John, do be careful."

Knowing they couldn't understand a word he said didn't stop him.

"Gentlemen, if you please. There is a perfectly good reason why this beautiful lady cannot come with you."

He stepped over to Aunt Polly and, to the delight of everyone, put his arm around her, saying in a loud voice, "Polly is *my* woman."

All Aunt Polly could manage to say was, "Why, John."

I'm sure my mouth dropped open, but before I could close it, Eli stood up and helped me to my feet. Looking straight into the braves' faces, he took my hand and said, "And Clarissa," he paused only for a second, "I hope, is *mine.*"

Without hesitating, I gave him a small nod.

The two Indians bowed their heads and rode slowly away, taking the blankets and ponies with them. We watched in silence until they went over a small hill and disappeared from sight.

I had no idea the size of the audience watching us until nearly half the camp began to clap and cheer.

"John," Captain Bennett said, "it's about time."

Aunt Polly came over to where we stood and wrapped the thick quilt around my shoulders, saying, "Clarissa, you must stay warm. I won't come so close to losing you ever again."

Eli held my hand up to his cheek and said, "Neither will I."

Two days later, we watched Eli gallop away to rejoin his company of elders. He promised to write to us as often as he could, and we would do the same. How different it felt this time to say good-bye, knowing that when he returned we would be together again.

We pulled our cart through the colorful slopes of Emigration Canyon with hearts so light that some of the people sang at the top of their lungs, while others shouted for joy.

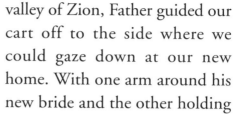

When we reached the crest overlooking the valley of Zion, Father guided our cart off to the side where we could gaze down at our new home. With one arm around his new bride and the other holding Andrew in front of him, he said, "There it is, family, the land of our dreams."

Aunt Polly rested her head on his shoulder.

Suddenly, rain began to sprinkle around us, making a light hushing sound on the grass.

Aunt Polly closed her eyes and lifted her face toward heaven, saying, "Don't you just love the smell of rain?"

At that moment, I knew for certain—we would all be very happy here.

# GLOSSARY
## In Clarissa's Own Words

**bartering**—Making a deal for something we needed when we had no money—making a trade. **See page 72.**

**bluff**—The steep side of a hill or mountain. **See page 58.**

**buffalo wallow**—A shallow pond or stream that the buffalo use for drinking and cooling themselves off. **See page 52.**

**bunions**—Swollen sores on the toe or foot. **See page 26.**

**codger**—An old fellow. **See page 38.**

**crosspiece**—The pulling bar at the front of the handcart. **See page 54.**

**croup**—An illness that includes a hoarse cough. A person with croup has a hard time breathing as well. **See page 26.**

**emetic**—A medicine that makes a person vomit. **See page 58.**

**fair game**—Free for someone to take as their own. **See page 54.**

**ferry**—A boat that carries people and, in our case, handcarts over a large river. **See page 24.**

**fry cake**—A breadlike food made from a light egg and flour dough that is fried. **See page 20.**

**grasshopper war**—The Saints in the Salt Lake Valley

were having a terrible time saving their crops from being eaten by grasshoppers. **See page 17.**

**grit**—Great courage and determination. **See page 30.**

**half a crown**—A silver English coin worth two shilling and six pence, or about 30 cents. **See page 4.**

**handcart**—A flat wooden box with two side wheels and a pulling handle out front. **See page 9.**

**"Handcart City"**—The camp three miles west of Iowa City where handcarts were built and the Saints made ready to move west. **See page 8.**

**Handcart Song**—We sang many songs on the trail, but the most popular of them all was the one which goes, "For some must push and some must pull, as we go marching up the hill. So merrily on our way we go, until we reach the valley-o." **See page 59.**

**horned toads**—Flat, round-sided lizards with two spiky horns on top of their head. **See page 37.**

**hub**—The center of a wheel. **See page 46.**

**Independence Rock**—A large rock that serves as a landmark for travelers in Wyoming. Pioneers and explorers often carve into the rock their names and the date they were there. **See page 42.**

**likenesses**—Sketches or pictures, drawn by hand, of someone or something. **See page 31.**

**lobelia**—A strong medicine used to stop pain and help a person sleep. **See page 58.**

**milch cow**—Another name for a milk cow. **See page 61.**

**neck bob**—A fancy ornament to hang around the neck. **See page 62.**

**Pawnee**—A tribe of Indians who live in the western plains. **See page 28.**

**peddler wagons**—The carts that peddlers loaded with goods to sell and pushed through the streets in England. **See page 14.**

**playing old gooseberry**—Making a mess of something. **See page 13.**

**poisoned**—Spoiled or ruined—or in Brother Folkman's case, sprayed by a skunk. **See page 38.**

**prattle**—Chatter or senseless talk. **See page 48.**

**rods**—One rod is about sixteen and a half feet, or five and a half yards. **See page 38.**

**Roman sandpit**—For their entertainment, the Romans used to make people fight in arenas. Sometimes they made people fight in water, mud, or sand. Aunt Polly meant that it felt like we were fighting our way through a deep, sandy hole. **See page 66.**

**saffron tea**—An orange tea made from the crocus flower. **See page 56.**

**tallowed cloth**—A waxed or greased cloth used to keep the sun from burning our lips any further. **See page 23.**

**thawing out**—A scolding or a serious talking to. **See page 44.**

**tongue**—The long wooden pole at the front of the wagon that the oxen are harnessed to. **See page 17.**

**tresses**—Locks of hair. **See page 12.**

**typhoid**—A deadly disease of fever and terrible stomach pain. **See page 25.**

**wolf ruckus**—A place where it was plain to see that a wolf or a pack of wolves had attacked something. **See page 57.**

**Yorkshire biscuits**—Light, fluffy biscuits made with eggs and butter. **See page 27.**

## What Really Happened

"At . . . one period, 1856–60, . . . nearly three thousand men, women and children, pulling their worldly possessions in hand-made, two-wheeled carts, trudged some thirteen hundred miles to the Zion of their hopes. Across prairies and mountains, rivers and deserts, creaked their fragile vehicles, motored by muscle and fueled with blood.

"There were blind and deaf; little children and infants in arms; gray veterans . . . ; old ladies and pregnant women.

"Babies were born on the journey; marriages were performed at the camps; old and young were buried along the trail. Overpowered by summer heat, [some] . . . fainted beside their carts. Scores froze in the biting cold of Wyoming blizzards. . . .

"From less than three thousand emigrants, who pulled or trailed a cart [more than] one hundred years ago, have come a half million

Americans. Cherishing a unique heritage, they are proud to claim descent from Handcart pioneers."

(LeRoy R. Hafen and Ann W. Hafen, *Handcarts to Zion,* [Glendale, Calif.: The Arthur H. Clark Co., 1960], 11–12.)

## About the Author

When Launi Anderson was approached with the idea of writing books for the Latter-day Daughters Series, she balked. "I only write picture books," she said. With more than 25,000 copies of her novels sold, she has proven that she can, indeed, write for the 8- to 12-year-old audience.

Launi is the mother of five children, April, Lyndi, Jillian, Dane, and Rhen. She has adopted a dog and owns an assortment of cats and one hedgehog.

Launi has had many callings in the Church. She says that one of the things she enjoys doing most is LDS historical research.

Not only does Launi write and play with her kids, but she also enjoys music, cooking, storytelling, organizing, and chatting. She is clever, witty, and a blast to be around. If you need a good laugh, find Launi. She's my friend.

Love,
Carol

**From *Victoria's Courage***
**Another Exciting New Title**
**in the Latter-day Daughters Series**

The house was rocking so hard that by the time I got to the window, I feared I might fall through and to the ground two stories below. Glass shattered, sending shards into my room. Had I been any closer, I would have been cut. My mirror fell over with a crash, and a rumble began to fill my ears. Plaster fell off the walls in chunks.

"Miss Polly," I cried, but there was no sound from her. Was everything strange happening only in *my* room, or was the whole *earth* rocking? I had to see for myself.

Never did it take me so long to get to the wall. At the window, I looked through the broken glass to the streets below. The earth rolled toward me as if the ground had changed from something solid to the waves of the ocean. The rumble, which grew louder with every second, seemed to roll with the earth.

I was thrown from my feet then.